CANDLISH

Louise Candlish is the *Sunday Times* bestselling author of *The Other Passenger* and thirteen other novels. *Our House* won the Crime & Thriller Book of the Year at the 2019 British Book Awards. It is now in development for a major TV series. Louise lives in London with her husband and daughter.

Thanks to your help, we're getting the nation reading!

1 in 6 adults in the UK struggles with reading. Buying this Quick Read could change someone's life.

For every Quick Read sold, a copy will be donated to someone who finds reading difficult. From mental health to social mobility, reading has a proven positive impact on life's big challenges. Find out more: readingagency.org.uk @readingagency #QuickReads

Also by Louise Candlish

LOUISE CANDLISH

the *skylight*

SIMON &
SCHUSTER

London · New York · Sydney · Toronto · New Delhi

First published in Great Britain by Simon & Schuster UK Ltd, 2021

1 3 5 7 9 10 8 6 4 2

Simon & Schuster UK Ltd
1st Floor
222 Gray's Inn Road
London WC1X 8HB

Simon & Schuster Australia, Sydney
Simon & Schuster India, New Delhi

www.simonandschuster.co.uk
www.simonandschuster.com.au
www.simonandschuster.co.in

A CIP catalogue record for this book
is available from the British Library

Paperback ISBN: 978-1-4711-9841-0
eBook ISBN: 978-1-4711-9842-7

Typeset in Stone Serif by M Rules
Printed and bound by CPI Group (UK) Ltd, Croydon, CR0 4YY

MIX
Paper from
responsible sources
FSC® C020471
FSC
www.fsc.org

the
skylight

Chapter 1

The cancelled dinner

Jake and I are having a special meal together tonight. Or I thought we were. But I have just spent my lunch hour shopping for food and wine when he phones to cancel me.

What a horrible word to apply to people – *cancel*. As if you no longer exist.

'What's the problem?' I say into the phone. I'm in the lift by now, going back up to the office. My shopping is heavy in my hand and I know there'll be a painful red mark across my palm.

'We've got a crisis with a job the new bloke has to deliver in the morning,' Jake sighs. He often moans about junior IT staff at the college where he works. 'He's just told me he's struggling to get it done and I can't just leave him on his own. You know how it is, Simone.'

Well, I know how it *was*. When we first started going out, Jake would happily leave younger co-workers to fend for themselves. It's six months since he moved into my flat and I feel as if we've grown further apart, not closer.

'Okay,' I tell him, nicely, though I'd like to drop the groceries to the floor and stamp on them. I feel a rash rising on my neck like a nettle sting. 'I might see if Paula wants to go for a drink after work.'

Paula is my cousin and the only member of my family I'm still in regular contact with.

'Good idea,' Jake says.

The lift doors open, and I step into the lobby of the housing charity where I've had a job in admin for as long as I can remember. Normally, I'm happy here, but suddenly I can't bear the thought of a long afternoon doing the same old thing.

'Don't wait up if you're back home first,' Jake says before he hangs up.

Paula isn't free after work and so I go straight home, arriving with my shopping at the usual time of a quarter to seven. My flat takes up the first and second floors of 17 Lyle Road, a quiet, red-brick street in Woking. I bought it when my dad died and left me enough for the deposit. I try not to think of how I owe my home to him, because that upsets my view that he ruined my life. I don't like to think *he* is what makes me lucky.

That's what the couple downstairs called me when they moved in. 'You're so *lucky* to have that big place all to yourself. We're totally jealous!'

They're called Gus and Alina and they are the perfect couple. They're younger than me – early thirties, I would say, and very good-looking. They are also very selfish. When they built their kitchen extension, they didn't once say sorry for the mess and noise. They acted like the whole house was theirs.

It was down to me to approach them. I chose Gus, because I'd taken an instant dislike to Alina – and she to me. 'I hope you'll make sure your builders only work the hours permitted by the council,' I said. He didn't even know what those hours were. So I printed off the page from the website and left it on the narrow table in the hallway.

There was a full year after that of vans parked at the gate, lorries pulling up and a dirty skip sitting right outside. Then, when it was finally finished, I had to put up with the smug way Alina asked friends in to show the place off. 'Come and see what our architect has done!' Like she was the Queen of Sheba.

She's never once invited me in.

Gus is away on a work trip tonight. I saw him getting into a taxi for the airport this morning.

He is a consultant, Alina told Jake – though I have no idea what he consults on. 'That's right, Terminal Five,' he said to the taxi driver, so loudly I heard him from the bedroom. Even at six in the morning in an empty street, he feels the need to act busy and important.

Alina is in. I know this even though the blind is closed on the bedroom window at the front. It is always closed, even at weekends. As I open the front door, I hear the clubby electronic music she likes. The beat of it is like a human pulse and makes me feel a bit sick.

I also have the start of a headache. For this reason, I wedge the bag of shopping in the fridge without unpacking it and go straight to the top floor to run a bath.

I'm the only one who uses this bathroom. Jake uses the shower room on the floor below – we agreed this when he moved in. It was my only condition, because it makes me ill to find other people's hairs in the bath or basin. Or tissues stained with bodily fluids on the floor by the pedal bin.

As I run the bath, I keep the light very low because my doctor says dazzle could affect my headaches. Also, I can see through the window better when there's no reflection from light inside the room. I peer down now into the skylight in the roof of Gus and Alina's extension – it's a huge stretch of glass, still all clean and new. There is no blind on it and the room is lit up, as it always is.

Directly below the skylight is a small white dining table. Every morning, when I'm brushing my teeth and washing my face, I only need glance down to view the couple's breakfast choices. Alina is a healthy eater and always has fruit and a bowl of muesli. She often reads the packets as she eats, no doubt checking her calorie count (she's very thin). Gus eats a fry-up or eggs on toast or other fattening things. I've seen her offer him the muesli box, put out an extra bowl and spoon for him, but he's not interested in her rabbit food.

It gives me a secret thrill to watch him defy her.

Because of the skylight, I know the tops of their heads better than their faces. The stripes of Alina's highlights running down from a centre parting. The way Gus's hand passes over his thinning hair, as if his touch will make the hair grow thick again.

There are no heads to see yet, but the table is already laid for dinner, a jug of pink roses at its centre. Alina must be having a friend over – God forbid she should be alone for a single evening. They have people over all the time, she and Gus.

On weekends, you see their friends squeezed around the table, dishes of food pushed from person to person. You see arms reaching into the middle and wine glasses meeting. *To us*, I imagine them saying. *To our perfect life.*

I should explain about the skylight and how they don't notice me watching. From down there, the glass in my window does not look clear. It has that one-way privacy film you often see on street-level windows – you can see out, but people can't see in. Gus and Alina don't realize this, but I actually think they'd like to know they are on display, their life in a spotlight. They'd be pleased to be openly envied.

Jake doesn't know either, in case you're wondering. As I said, he never uses my bathroom. It's my one condition.

Besides, if he knew I was spying, he would only tell me not to do it.

I usually like my bath very hot, but tonight I keep the water cool because of the headache. I don't want to faint and drown. That was the thing I disliked most about living alone, the risk of not being found if you had an accident. As I slide my shoulders underwater, I hear the ring on the doorbell below and then the slam of the front door.

You can't hear voices from up here, but it's easy to imagine Alina greeting her guest. 'So fab to see you! Let's crack this bottle open!' Next time I look, I'll see one of her silly girlfriends at the table, sloshing back the wine. Like her, they work in the fashion industry and dress in clothes that are fluffy or metallic or crinkled. The kind of outfits the rest of us wouldn't be seen dead in.

This thought makes me look down at my naked body in the bath and I think, *We all die. This body will one day be a corpse.* Morbid, I know. I should enjoy every minute of life while I have it. Life is the most precious thing in our universe and we must respect it above all else. That's what it says on the websites Paula recommends. *Manage your mind, Simone. Have a positive mental outlook.*

No more negative thoughts, I decide. If Jake has to work and miss our special dinner, that's that. No big deal. If Alina is young and pretty and popular, good for her.

I pull myself out of the water and put on my bathrobe. Maybe I'll clean my teeth and go straight to bed. Sleep off the headache. But first I make a final check on the scene below.

As I expected, two figures are now at the table, both holding glasses of red wine. The roses have been moved and there is a platter of vegetable batons in their place, plus the wine bottle. Alina is in her usual spot, facing out to the garden. Her blonde hair is piled on top of her head and her shoulders are bare and tanned, even though it's a winter evening.

My gaze moves to her guest. He is sitting in Gus's seat, his back a little stiff, like it's a date. As he tips his head up a little, I can see his glasses, the curve of his cheekbones and his rosy skin. Alina must have said something funny because he's laughing.

Laughing harder than he ever does at anything *I* say.

What's so funny, Jake?

Chapter 2

The first time

Once I stop gasping with shock, I try to think of a simple reason for this. Maybe Jake finished work earlier than expected and decided to surprise me. He bumped into Alina in the hallway, and now finds himself sitting at her table against his wishes. He is itching to escape her healthy snacks and come upstairs to me.

But, hang on, he rang her doorbell, didn't he? He arrived at the front door and rang her bell. Did he think a knock on her flat door wouldn't be heard over the music?

Did he cancel me to see her?

It's easy enough to find out. I fetch my phone from the bedroom and text him:

I'm at Paula's. Join us if you finish soon?

Through the skylight, I watch him fish in his pocket for his phone. He doesn't think to glance up. Why would he? I told him I'd be staying out and even if he did look up, all he'd see is a blank window.

He places his phone on the table, screen facing down, and picks up his glass again.

The message arrives:

No chance, still at work.

I hear myself moan. So he has purposely lied to me. Deceived me. Tonight of all nights, when he knew I was cooking a special meal. And not only that, but he had no way of knowing I would say I would go and see Paula. He was willing to take the risk of bumping into me because he wanted to visit Alina so much.

My breath feels thin and frantic as I go on watching for as long as they go on sitting at the table. After the raw veggies, a dish of something stew-like arrives, but they don't seem to eat much of it. Too busy drinking and laughing. When they move from the table, I tighten the belt of my robe and creep down the stairs to listen at Alina's door.

I can't hear much because of the music. There are murmurs between songs, but no distinct words. If I hadn't seen Jake through the skylight, I would have no way of knowing he was in there.

Has he done this before or is it the first time?

It's cold in the hallway and I shiver. After a while, I hear their voices come closer. I guess they are moving to the bedroom at the front. I hear Jake say, 'You are unbelievable.' And Alina answers, 'I know.' Two sets of groans. Alina's giggles. The scuffling sound of bodies against the wall. The closing of a door – the bedroom door, I guess. More groans.

I wait in the hallway till they go quiet. I stand there for a long time, maybe half an hour, before opening the main front door and closing it again with a thump. Then I hurry up the stairs as if I've just arrived home.

I text Jake:

Back home. Headache.

It's almost half past ten. I wonder when he'll fake *his* return. Or maybe he'll text me to say he's pulling an all-nighter in the office.

In the flat, I turn on the kitchen light, run the tap for a glass of water, turn the TV on loud. Make it clear I am home in case he hasn't seen the text. But when I go to bed at midnight, he still hasn't come up.

At twelve-thirty, I hear the main house door open and close. I picture Alina watching him from her doorway like the cat that got the cream. Then I hear his footsteps on the stairs and the key in our door.

He doesn't come straight up, but uses his shower room below. It's another fifteen minutes before he's in the bedroom and slipping into bed next to me. Our legs touch and I can feel the dampness of his skin. I can smell how clean he is.

I think I won't sleep, but I do, dreaming of my mum and the way she cried and cried when my dad walked out and started a new life with his colleague Suzi. Mum didn't get angry and try to fight for him, she just cried.

I was only eleven years old, but she left me to fight her battles for her.

In the morning, I feel surprisingly powerful. I suppose we all like knowing something other people don't know we know.

'Did you get your job done?' I ask Jake. It is clear to me that life must go on normally between us while I decide on my next move. Questions about work, that's normal. Making us both toast and peanut butter, that's normal too, even if I do feel like spitting on his. 'Who was it who screwed up?'

'Dev,' he says, smooth as anything. 'I told him

this is the last time I save his skin, but I don't suppose it will be.'

I study him as he talks about the big meeting he has today. Does he look different? Like his life is suddenly more exciting? His sandy hair is sticking out on one side, slept on wet, but other than that he is the same. Like me, Jake is not beautiful. He looks decent, earnest. *I* love him, but it's hard to know why Alina is interested.

He eats the toast with smacking sounds, as if he's starving.

'Are you all right, Simone?' he says.

I smile. 'Absolutely fine.'

'Are you cross about dinner? I'm really sorry I had to bail.'

'It's no problem. I wasn't feeling that well, anyway.'

'Oh yes, you had a headache. Poor thing. What time did you get home?'

'Ten-thirty or eleven.'

'Did you get a cab from the station?' His tone is casual but I can tell he's thinking he didn't hear a taxi pull up. He was in Alina's bedroom at the time and he surely would have heard. I wonder if Alina changed the bedclothes before her 'date' with my boyfriend. Or was she happy to use the same sheets Gus had slept on the night before?

'No,' I say. 'I walked.'

'Through the short cut?' Our eyes meet and I see that he still cares. He doesn't want me walking alone down short cuts late at night. He still loves me.

He leaves for work first and I watch from behind the living room curtains. I wonder if he and Alina have made a plan to meet at the station. But I've forgotten that she drives to work in her shiny yellow Fiat 500. Here she comes, dressed as if for a party in flared white jeans and a big fake-fur jacket.

Before she gets into the car, she glances up at my window and pauses. I don't like the look on her face – like she's the winner, the champion. What did Jake say just now? *I told him this is the last time, but I don't suppose it will be.* Does that mean he and Alina plan to see each other again?

Suddenly, I see what's going on here. Stealing Jake is another way of making it known to me that I don't count. She's taken him just because she can, like Jolene in the song Mum played over and over when Dad left.

I need to teach her a lesson.

Chapter 3

Happy anniversary!

I am the first home from work that evening. The post is scattered on the doormat and I sort it into two lots, one for each flat. There are three pieces of mail for Jake and me – our monthly phone bills and a catalogue of hiking gear for Jake – and four for Gus and Alina, whose surname is Hunt. 'The Hunts', one of their envelopes says. It looks like a posh invitation and I add it to my own pile before heading upstairs.

In the kitchen, I do exactly what I planned to do yesterday. Prepare the pepper sauce for the steaks, slice the potatoes for fries, mix the dressing for the salad. Light the candles and open the wine. I remember Alina's roses and wish I had something pretty for the table. For now, I put a small potted fern in their spot.

Jake arrives at 7.45pm, and we sit down to dinner exactly twenty-four hours late for our original date. He attacks his plate with a lot more appetite than I saw last night when he had a bowl of Alina's veggie mush in front of him. But then he wasn't there for the food, was he?

'You didn't have to cook tonight instead, you know,' he says.

'I'd already shopped when you cancelled. Then I lugged it all the way to Paula's and back here,' I say, remembering the lie. 'No point wasting it.'

Gus is back from his trip. When I looked through the skylight half an hour ago, I saw his overnight bag on the table. He doesn't know what his wife got up to in his absence, but *I* do.

'Okay then. I'm pleased you did.' Jake raises his wine glass and touches it against mine. 'Happy anniversary!'

Two years. Not of marriage, of course, but of being together. I'd hoped he might propose to me last night, but instead he was sleeping with someone else's wife.

The invitation I took from downstairs was to a wedding. It's in the kitchen bin now, torn into pieces. It's possible Gus and Alina won't be joining their friends Pippa and Simon on 14 June to celebrate the joy of their union.

Personally, I think the occasion will be better without them.

*

16

I'm tempted to hang back when I next see them, but I force myself to say hello. It is Saturday afternoon and they are leaving the house as I am arriving home from a ten-thousand-step walk. I always go for a walk on Saturday afternoon.

'Hi, Simone,' Gus says. He looks very handsome in a wool suit and crisp white shirt. Alina is in an animal-print coat, with sunglasses in her hair, even though it's not sunny. Curls of silky blonde hair sit on her shoulders like golden snakes.

'Hi, Gus. Hi, Alina. Off somewhere smart?'

'A big fortieth birthday,' Gus says. 'One of my clients.'

It seems to me that Alina's smile is a little sly. Even beautiful people look ugly when they do bad things. When they are cheats. I wonder what she'd say if I told her husband, 'Alina had sex with Jake the night you were away.' He'd be so shocked – and so would she.

'Well, enjoy yourselves,' I say. 'Forty comes to us all.' This isn't true, so I add, 'Unless you're unlucky enough to die young.'

'What a thing to say, Simone,' Alina replies, smirking.

After the door is closed between us, there is silence as they make their way into the street. Then I hear a huge bellow of Gus's laughter, which I know means she has made some cruel remark about me. Maybe that was what she was doing when she made Jake laugh that night.

It seems to me that women like her need to learn what pain feels like.

Now I've seen it done once, I know what to look out for. Another work trip for Gus, another late night for Jake pulling a project together. All hands on deck.

This time it is a trip to the cinema that he cancels. 'Sorry, Simone,' he says. 'You go on your own, don't waste the tickets.'

'I'd rather go with you,' I say. 'I'll get a refund.'

He doesn't seem bothered by the thought of me being at home for the evening. I suppose it is easy enough for him to scan the street and avoid arriving at the door at the same time as me. To change his plan if he *does* bump into me. Then, once inside her flat, door closed, he knows as well as I do you can't hear voices from upstairs.

But to be on the safe side, Alina has turned the music up again.

I watch through the skylight with the same attention I would pay to a TV show. They are only at the table for a few minutes this time, clearly not eating a proper meal. Just a bowl of what look like vegetable crisps. A bottle of white wine. After an hour, I go down and knock at her door.

'Simone!' The shock on her face is comical. At least she is fully clothed, though her heavy make-up is smudged.

'Did I startle you?' I say, pleasantly.

'No, yes. I mean, I thought you were going to be our builder.'

At this time of night? You'd have thought she'd have come up with something better than that. 'Nice of them to work so late.'

'Or not, as the case may be.' She's calmed herself enough to make it sound as if this is my fault.

'Maybe give them a call,' I say, sweetly.

Throughout this, she keeps the door half closed and I imagine Jake inside, stock still at the sound of my voice. I can almost hear him willing Alina, *Get rid of her*.

'Was there something you wanted, Simone?'

'Yes, would you mind turning the music down? It's very loud and I'm having an early night.'

'Of course. No problem.'

There's no apology, just a prompt closing of the door in my face.

With my ear against the frame, I make out her voice, 'Just the music.' Then, when the volume is lowered, murmurs followed by a slammed door.

It's an odd thing, feeling a sense of victory

when your worst fears are confirmed. Like you've won and lost at the same time.

Jake doesn't come up for another two hours.

For every time I'm aware of Jake cheating on me, I take a piece of Alina's mail. It's a petty kind of revenge, just something small while I think of a bigger, better plan.

I always choose something personal. She has a lot of invitations, postcards from a friend in Italy, thank-you cards after dinner parties. Taking a speeding ticket gives me a thrill. If she doesn't fill in the form, she'll get six points on her licence. That will annoy her. I rip up the form from the Surrey Police and put it in the bin.

It's not long before she notices and moans to Jake about it.

'I just saw Alina in the hall,' he tells me, one evening.

'Oh yes? How is our local mean girl?'

'Simone,' he protests.

'Well, she is.'

'I'm sure she's okay underneath it all.'

What, without her clothes on, I think. I wonder if he'll defend her any more than that, but he's not stupid.

'She said they think post has been going missing,' he says.

'Really? I haven't noticed anything.'

'Me neither, but I suppose you only notice if you're expecting something and it doesn't arrive. Just in case, she asked if we can double-check the main door is closed properly every time we go in and out.'

'I always do,' I say, in exactly the offended way Jake would expect.

Chapter 4

The plan

On the seventh or eighth time, I finally find something useful in the mail. It's an NHS-branded envelope addressed to 'A.F. Hunt'. (I wonder what her middle name is – I can offer a few rude suggestions.) Upstairs, I open it at the kitchen table with a nice cup of green tea. It's from the allergy clinic of a big London hospital, confirming a set of tests. It says that a severe allergy to Brazil nuts has already been found and all tree nuts 'strictly removed from the patient's diet'. But minor symptoms persist and more tests are needed.

This must be the root of Alina's healthy eating. The reason she prepares everything herself and checks all the packets. Even the muesli that she's eaten for as long as I've been watching – every time she opens a new box, she checks again. Perhaps she fears they've changed the recipe.

Mistakes happen all the time with allergies – there are always stories in the media.

And I think I might have a plan.

I know I must leave no trace on my phone or laptop. No research into allergies, no online grocery order history. Instead, I buy a bag of mixed nuts as part of my weekly supermarket shop and then I serve them in a bowl for snacking in front of the TV.

All except the Brazil nuts.

In the back of the cupboard is a spice grinder, a Christmas present from years ago never taken out of its box. If Jake was ever aware it was there, he will have forgotten. He didn't even notice when I bought a new kettle. One night, when making dinner, I grind the Brazil nuts and transfer the powder into a plastic bag, which I store in a Tupperware container.

The next day, I dispose of the grinder in a bin near the station.

Then I wait.

Early one morning, about two weeks later, the van of a posh building firm pulls up at the house and two workers ring Gus and Alina's doorbell. Listening from the stairs, I gather that the skylight has sprung a leak and they are here to do repairs. Gus has already left for work and Alina is telling the workmen about keys.

'If you leave them just here on this lamp table, that will be fine,' she says.

I phone my boss Martin and say I have one of my headaches and will try to get in later. Then I gather the bag of nut powder, a pair of rubber gloves and my phone, and I wait on the stairs for the right moment.

It couldn't work out better. The workers have propped open the downstairs flat door to bring in their ladders, leaving the place just long enough for me to slip through the door and into the bedroom. I close the bedroom door behind me and wait for my eyes to adjust to the dark – the blinds are the black-out kind and, as usual, haven't been opened.

I need to find somewhere to hide myself in case one of the builders decides to come into the room. The bed is high off the ground, with a huge bamboo headboard. If I sit behind it in the corner, I doubt I could be seen from the door, especially in this dim light.

The bed isn't made, the duvet hanging off one side. I imagine Alina and Jake rolling about on it and my anger deepens.

It's not as easy as you'd think to sit completely still and quiet. I use my phone – our own Wi-Fi works down here – though of course I keep it on silent. I catch snatches of chat between the workmen as they pass in the hallway, boring stuff about kids' gaming habits and football scores. I know better than to give in to the urge to peek in the bedside drawer or wardrobe. One squeak and I could be found.

I'm there for almost three hours. Then, at last, the builders phone Alina to give her the news that the leak has been fixed. Yes, her spare key will be left in the agreed spot. The flat door opens and closes, then the front door. The gate squeaks, van doors slam, and then the engine starts up.

Finally.

I stand up and ease my stiff muscles. Then I put on my rubber gloves and slip out of the bedroom and down the corridor to the extension. It's a huge, light space with a pale marble floor and an enormous sea-green sofa splitting the living room from the kitchen.

On the wall are dozens of framed photographs from fashion shoots. There is also a picture of Alina and Gus on their wedding day, the same size print in the same kind of frame, as if they are models too. In the kitchen, light floods through the skylight onto the glossy white units. The familiar tabletop stands on a slim white pedestal. It's weird to see it from a new angle.

There is no sign of repair to the skylight – perhaps the builders had to climb onto the roof. From here my bathroom window is a fully visible rectangle of what looks like dull reflective glass. There is no way you could know there was someone behind, watching.

Still wearing my gloves, I find Alina's box of muesli on the kitchen counter. 'Nut-free and 100% organic!', the brand promises. The box is heavy and for a moment I fear it hasn't been opened. I'll either have to give up on the project, or take the risk that she won't remember having started the new pack.

But then I see it *has* been opened, the flap tucked neatly into place. I ease it open with care and pour my powdered Brazil nuts into the mix. Then I close the box again and give it a good shake. I have no idea what dose is needed to bring on an attack, but I like the idea of Alina being very ill at least for a week or two. Far too weak to carry on her affair with Jake. Gus will care for her. He'll hardly let her out of his sight.

Job done, I'm careful not to leave fingerprints on the door as I leave, and I move as quietly as when I arrived. I admit I hover by Alina's keys, wonder about going to the key cutters on the high street and getting them copied. But that's quite a risk – someone might remember me.

Back in my own flat, I can't see the muesli box from the window. It already seems impossible that I was ever down there, trespassing. Planting a toxic substance in someone's breakfast cereal. I'm shaking from the adrenalin and, when it drains, I have a headache. I let Martin know that I won't be in after all. Later, I take a walk and throw away the nut bag, the Tupperware and the gloves in a bin on the high street.

The post has arrived by the time I get back and I take an item for Alina, addressed by hand and with a Central London postmark. When I open it, I find a small piece of paper with a short message on it and for a minute or two my heart leaps wildly in my chest. Once it feels normal again, I take a match to the note and burn it to ash. But I can't forget the words I just read:

I know this is you.

Chapter 5

Breakfast at Alina's

Gus and Alina come home together at eight and I see them looking up at the skylight, trying to judge if the work has been done. The sky is grey and heavy and they're probably willing it to rain so they can test the repairs. I'm not so keen on the idea. When it rains, the glass blurs and you can't see through it as clearly any more. You can only guess what's happening below.

It remains dry for dinner time. There's a vegetable stir-fry in a big shiny wok and little bowls of rice for them both. Gus has a beer, Alina a glass of wine.

Obviously, no one's going to eat muesli until morning.

I'm so keyed up for breakfast, I hardly sleep that night.

I'm up early, watching, but they don't appear. It's the weekend and they're lying in.

By 10.45, there's still no sign of them – at this rate they'll miss breakfast altogether!

Jake taps on my bathroom door. 'Are you still in there, Simone?'

'Having a bath,' I call. 'I'll be out in a minute.'

Eventually, after eleven, Gus and Alina appear and start making brunch. They have pancakes with berries and whipped cream, a rare treat for her. She eats just one pancake and Gus scoffs the rest. Then they sit with their coffee and phones.

The muesli isn't touched.

They are away on Saturday night and so there are no more meals at home this weekend. Finally, on the Monday morning, Alina returns to her usual breakfast. She pours a small bowl from the packet I've tampered with and adds milk from a fancy carton. Oat or soya, I guess. Certainly not almond or hazelnut.

I watch, hardly able to breathe. I expect her to start choking straightaway and Gus to leap from his seat and rush to her side. He'll call for an ambulance and I'll watch from the window as she's taken away on a stretcher. I can't help thinking about Suzi all those years ago, the panic on her face as she got in my dad's car, pulling up her knees in pain.

You stay here, Simone! I'm taking her to A&E!

But none of that happens. Alina simply spoons the muesli into her mouth till the bowl is empty and then clears it out of view. When she comes back, she has a banana in her hand. She's gesturing to Gus's plate – he's eating what looks like a sausage roll – and then she dips to kiss him on the top of his head. The next thing, the front door is closing and I hear the sound of her car starting up.

Clearly, the effects of the nut must be delayed. Will she start to feel ill in the car? So ill that she crashes? That in itself wouldn't be terrible, but I don't want anyone else to be hurt by this. Only *her*.

Whatever occurs, it is not serious enough for her to behave any differently, because she is back at the table that evening, eating dinner. I try to understand what has happened – or why it *hasn't* happened. Maybe I shook the box too hard, so the tiny portion she ate contained too little nut. Or perhaps the nuts lost their potency in the long period since they were ground. Or Alina's allergy is less chronic than the hospital letter led me to believe.

I've shredded the letter, of course. I'm not that stupid.

No, she is her usual sly self that evening. I actually watch her send the text to Jake that proposes their next meeting. I know that's what it is, because ten minutes later he tells me he's going to work from home in the morning. A morning session? That's new. Gus must be leaving early.

You'd think I might be relieved that my plan has failed, but I'm not.

I'm livid.

In the morning, I hear Gus run out to a taxi at seven and I pretend to leave for work at my usual time of eight.

'Don't forget we've got Paula for dinner tonight,' Jake says, which means can I start thinking about what to shop for, what to cook.

'Maybe you can cook,' I say to him, sharper than usual.

'Okay. If you don't mind the plunge in quality,' he laughs.

You're in a good mood, I think.

When I leave, I close the main door behind me before waiting on the doorstep, right at the side so I can't be seen through the glass panel. Luckily, I don't have to wait long before I hear Jake's heavy tread on the stairs. I set 'record' on my phone just in time to catch his knock at Alina's door.

'Hello, you.' Her voice is sultry, like a cartoon character.

'Hello, you.' He sounds like him, but younger. Cheekier. 'Gus has left, yeah?'

'Ages ago. What about her?'

'Just gone.'

'Good.'

There's at least a sense of tact in Jake's voice, if not shame, but hers is full of relish. The way she says, 'What about her?' as if I'm dirt.

She offers him coffee, and he's joking about taking it black because he doesn't like her oat milk. I wish I'd put the Brazil nut in *that* instead of the muesli. It might have worked by now.

Her door closes and I stop recording. I head down the path with silent steps, careful not to swing the gate and make it creak.

Chapter 6

Paula's visit

I always feel better when I see Paula. She's the only person left from my childhood who is aware of my story. My parents are both dead and my brother, Matt, moved to Spain five years ago. We weren't close, anyway.

I know I'm lucky that Paula works as a therapist and is always caring and discreet. She's never told a soul about what I did when I was eleven. As for Jake, she knows I've told him I went off the rails a bit when Mum and Dad split up, but that's all.

I go down and meet her at the front door. 'If Jake mentions us meeting after work a few weeks ago, can you go along with it?'

'Why, what's up?' she asks.

'I'm not sure yet. But can you?'

'Of course.'

As it turns out, Jake doesn't mention it. He's forgotten and is busy with cooking, anyway.

I wish I hadn't warned her, because now she's dying to ask me about it and know what the drama is. When I excuse myself to use the loo, she follows me up and is waiting outside the bathroom door when I come out.

'Paula! You gave me a fright.'

She giggles. 'Come in here.'

She steers me into the bedroom. 'Why did you tell Jake you were meeting me that time when you weren't?'

I sigh. 'Because I was doing something I don't want him to know about.'

Her mouth gapes with shock. 'Oh my God, I would never in a million years have predicted this!'

'Predicted what?'

'You're having an affair.'

I frown. '*I'm* not, no.'

'You mean Jake is?'

'Yes.'

Her shock turns to doubt. 'I don't believe that, Simone. He's not that kind of person. He's too ...'

'Nice? That's what I thought.' Talking about it with her is making me a bit shaky. I feel my anger with Alina growing. Alina didn't have muesli for breakfast this morning. She had a bowl of fruit salad, but it hardly matters now what she has. The top layer had the most ground nut in it so if that didn't work, the layers underneath definitely won't.

'I have proof,' I tell Paula.

'What proof?'

I don't want to let on about the skylight, so I tell her about the doorstep recording.

She frowns. 'You probably shouldn't have recorded a private conversation.'

'It's only a few seconds.' If she thinks the recording is bad, what would she say about the nuts? Sneaking into someone's flat and trying to poison their food! She'd say I was crazy and dangerous.

She'd mention what I did before.

'What are you going to do next?' she asks.

'I'll give him a few weeks and if he's still sneaking about, I'll confront him with the recording,' I say. 'I'll tell him he has to choose which of us he wants.'

'A few weeks?' Paula repeats. 'That's quite a long time to sit on it. You know, maybe he's not right for you if he's able to do this?'

'He *is* right for me,' I say.

'Okay.' Paula gives me a hug. 'I know it hurts, but these things happen and lots of couples get past it. If you want to talk about it, I'm here for you.'

We go back down and eat the terrible pasta dish Jake has served up. It's full of overcooked vegetables and I long to ask if he got the recipe from Alina.

When Paula leaves, I walk her to her car and she whispers, 'I had a thought. If *you* know about this, maybe her boyfriend knows as well? If they're meeting in their flat, they might have left clues.'

'Husband, not boyfriend,' I correct her.

'Husband. Maybe he'll find out and put an end to it and you won't have to do anything.'

'Oh.' I hadn't thought of that. I can't believe Gus does know, but maybe he should.

And it's Alina herself who's given me the idea of how I might tell him.

It is two more mornings before she leaves for work earlier than him. As soon as I see her car pull away, I slip down to the hall and place an envelope on the doormat, as if it's been posted through the letterbox. It is addressed to Mr G. Hunt. Inside is a piece of notepaper with one line printed on it:

Your wife is having an affair with the neighbour upstairs.

I've signed it, *A friend.*

Back in the flat, at the bathroom window, I see Gus sitting at the table with a fresh pot of coffee. The muesli box is still on the table from Alina's breakfast, along with her used bowl and his plate for the left-over pizza he ate. Pizza for breakfast! What did Alina think of that? And is it safe for the partner of someone with allergies to bring highly processed foods into the kitchen?

If I wait long enough, he might poison her for me!

Outside, the wind picks up and it starts to rain. I turn back to the mirror and add a smear of make-up on the rash that's appeared on my neck. I wonder if Gus will open my note in the hallway or slip it in his pocket to look at on the train.

I've changed my handwriting in case he recognizes it from notes I've left in the past about things like the building works and bins. I don't want Gus to say, 'Oh, well, if it's from Simone, I'll just ignore it.' I decide to wait a few minutes, in case he does open it and comes looking for Jake. I'll invite him in and tell him what I know.

Glancing a final time before I leave the bathroom, I freeze in horror. Though the skylight is dotted with rain, the glass is still clear enough for me to see Gus lying on his side on the kitchen floor. And he's not moving – he looks unconscious. Did he fall somehow and hit his head on that marble floor?

I open the window and stick my head out to shout down. 'Gus! Gus!' But he remains completely still. A dog barks from a garden a few doors down.

I dash downstairs and hammer on his door, before it strikes me as a useless plan. I know he's the only one home. I grab my phone and dial 999.

'My neighbour's fallen and knocked himself out. I think he might have a head injury!'

'Do you have a key to the flat?' they ask me.

'No.'

'Is there anyone who does, so we can talk you through how to help him while you wait?'

'No, no. I'm sorry. Please hurry!'

'Try to stay calm. Someone will be there in a few minutes,' they promise.

I wait on the stairs, clutching my phone, trying not to think of poor Gus. Only when I hear help arrive – police as well as ambulance – and watch officers break down the door, do I remember to snatch back my note from the hall table.

Chapter 7

Sad news

Gus is on a stretcher being carried to the ambulance in the drizzle. A plastic mask has been placed over his face and his skin is a strange pale grey. I tell the paramedic I will contact Alina and let her know what has happened. A police officer is going to stay in their flat to wait for someone to come and fix the broken door.

I'm finding it hard to process what is happening, and so it's a few minutes before I realize I don't actually know how to get in touch with Alina. We have never swapped phone numbers.

I ring Jake. 'Something's happened to Gus. I phoned for an ambulance and I need to let Alina know where he is. Can you remember who she works for? It's a fashion PR, but I can't remember the name.'

'What?' Jake is shocked. 'What do you mean? What's happened to Gus?'

'I think he fell and knocked himself out. I was opening the bathroom window and I saw him through the skylight. They've taken him to hospital.'

'Bloody hell, that's terrible! Thank God you saw it or he might still be lying there!'

An idea suddenly strikes. 'I think he must have climbed onto a chair to look at the skylight. It was raining and maybe it was leaking again?'

'I have no idea,' Jake says. 'Leave it with me, I'll phone Alina.'

'You have her number?'

There is a pause. 'No, but I know who she works for. I'll look them up.'

I give him the hospital details and then hang up. From the bathroom window I look down, wondering if I'll see the police officer. The rain has stopped and I can view the scene more clearly. The couple's breakfast things are still on the table, and I see now what I couldn't see when I was focusing on poor Gus. Next to the plate with pizza crust on his side of the table is a bowl of what looks like muesli. A spoon lies on the floor, near where Gus fell. It can't have anything to do with his fall, but it makes me feel uneasy, and I have a strong desire to go into the flat and take a closer look.

When the urge won't go away, I head back down. Though the lock is broken, I don't dare walk straight in. So I use the outside bell to call the officer.

'Simone.' She has remembered my name. 'I thought you were going to work?'

I nod. 'I was, but I wondered, would you like *me* to stay and arrange for a locksmith?'

That way I can have a proper look around.

'Thank you,' she says, 'but it's all in hand. I'll stay here until it's secure. I'm expecting other colleagues, as well. You get yourself off to work.'

What does she mean, 'other colleagues'? I don't dare ask.

I have no choice but to do as she says.

In the office, it seems amazing that other people's mornings are just normal – even boring. Martin tries to tell me off for my lateness, but I give my excuses with a tear in my eye. 'Would you like to speak to the police to confirm it? If you don't believe me?'

He changes his tune. 'Of course I believe you, Simone. Well done, it sounds like you were a real hero!'

I tell the story to other co-workers and start to believe Martin is right. 'Is there any news on your neighbour?' they keep asking.

'No,' I say, 'but I'm sure he'll be fine. He's in safe hands.' I feel quite popular.

I'm allowed to leave work early and arrive home by five-thirty. The Hunts' flat is quiet and a new lock has been fitted. The police officer has gone.

I'm too nervous to eat, but start preparing dinner for something to do. I've left several messages for Jake to ask if he was able to track down Alina, but it's close to six-thirty by the time he phones back.

'Where are you?' I ask.

'I'm still at the hospital with Alina.'

'Why?'

'Because she needs someone with her, that's why.' He pauses. 'Simone, I have some bad news about Gus. Really bad news.'

'What do you mean?' I hold my breath.

'He's died. Gus has died. I meant to phone you earlier, but there's been so much to do . . .'

'I don't understand.' This can't be right. I've misheard him. 'I called for help.'

He must sense my shock because he speaks very soothingly, as if to a child. 'It was good that you called the ambulance and Alina's very grateful, but he went into cardiac arrest at the hospital and they couldn't save him.'

'Was it . . . was it a head injury? I told you they just had their skylight fixed, so maybe he'd—'

'No,' Jake says. 'There was a swelling on his

head from the fall, but that wasn't how he died. He had an attack of anaphylaxis – that's an allergic reaction.'

I go cold. 'Allergic reaction? What to?'

'He had a severe allergy to certain nuts, apparently.'

'I don't understand,' I repeat.

'Alina says Brazil nuts are the worst, but she's really strict about having any trace of nuts in their kitchen. They buy most things from a special website. Even the pizza that she thinks was the last thing he ate came from this special nut-free brand.'

I can't speak. It makes no sense. Why did the hospital letter come for Alina if it was Gus who had the allergy?

But I can't ask Jake that. 'I didn't know he had an allergy,' I say, finally.

'Why would you? Look, Alina's going to stay with a friend tonight and I said I'd drive her over in her car.'

'But you're not insured,' I protest.

'Then I'm going to break the law for twenty minutes. All right?' He sounds very stressed out. 'I have to go. I'll be home as soon as I've handed her over to her friend.'

'Okay.' I put down the phone and cover it with my hands, as if that will change the news. I have made a terrible mistake and now I must keep a terrible secret.

I have killed someone.

For the next ten minutes, I sit at the kitchen table with one hand pressed to my mouth to stop myself from wailing. Then I pull myself together and start checking my phone. I delete the recording I made of Jake and Alina talking. I scan my texts, but there is nothing suspicious. The only person I've told about the affair is Paula, and I know she will protect me if push comes to shove.

I remember that the note to Gus is still in my pocket and I tear it into tiny pieces. All the mail I stole is already destroyed.

I give the kitchen worktops and floor another deep clean and throw the cloths I've used in the bin.

By the time I've done all this, Jake comes home. We hug and I smell the hospital on him. I wonder if he saw Gus's dead body.

'It's awful,' I say. 'I can't believe it.'

'Nor can I,' Jake says. 'Alina's in a bad way. She blames herself.'

'Why?'

'Because she's the one who does all the food shopping. Like I told you, she buys these special brands. She checks the ingredients in everything.'

'She must have missed something,' I say, and he gives me a sharp look. Was my tone wrong? Too uncaring? 'You said something about pizza?' I add.

'Yes. Alina thought that was the last thing he ate, but the police say he was eating muesli when the attack happened.'

I go very cold.

'But Alina's sure there were no Brazil nuts in it or nuts of any kind, so God knows what it was.'

'Then it must have been one of those freak things,' I suggest. 'You know, a trace of something in the factory from another product?'

'Maybe.' Jake rubs his eyes and I see how pink and tired they are. 'The police have taken the pizza packaging and a sample of the muesli, so we'll find out as soon as they've done their tests and examined the contents of his stomach.'

I feel the blood drain from my face, but he doesn't seem to notice. He's too busy worrying about Alina.

Chapter 8

Police questions

It is a few days before Alina comes home. I slip out to buy flowers and then knock at her door.

'Simone. Hi.' She looks really terrible, with swollen eyes and lank hair, and she wears grey, sloppy clothes – more like mine than hers.

'I'm so sorry for your loss,' I say, offering the flowers.

'Thank you.'

'Do you know any more about how it happened? Jake said it might have been an allergic reaction?'

'It was. They found Brazil nut in our muesli. Brazil nut that wasn't supposed to be there.'

I blink. *Oh God.*

'The police just had me in today for questioning, actually,' she goes on. 'They seem to think I added nut to the muesli, knowing he would go into anaphylactic shock.'

'No one would do that,' I cry. It's clear now

how lucky I was that the police officer didn't let me into the flat to sort out the locksmith. Clearing up and throwing out the muesli would have been a clear sign of my guilt. Now it is much more likely that the person who knew about the allergy in the first place is guilty.

'I know, it's a crazy idea, like something out of an Agatha Christie.' Alina pauses, a bleak look on her face. 'Anyway, my solicitor thinks there's no way the police can bring a charge of any kind. I just want it all cleared up so we can organize the funeral. I can't bear to think of Gus in the morgue. In limbo.'

She begins to cry and I don't know what to say. 'Would you like to come up for a cup of tea?' I suggest, at last.

'No, I just want to ... Thank you for the flowers, that was very nice of you.'

'Please just say if there's anything I can do.'

'Actually ...' She bites her lower lip, shifts her gaze. 'If you wouldn't mind sending Jake down when he gets home. I'd really like to get his advice on what the police said.'

'Of course,' I say, warmly.

I repeat this to Jake when he returns. 'I've never been her greatest fan, but even I can see you need a motive to try to kill your husband.

Then again, you never really know what's going on with a couple, do you? Behind closed doors. Maybe he was abusive to her.'

Jake frowns. 'Of course he wasn't abusive.'

'Perhaps he was cheating, then?'

His eyes go very wide.

'Or there could have been something to do with money,' I add. I'm getting nervous. 'Bad debts that were causing tension?'

'Bad debts?' He begins to look cross. 'You didn't share these ideas with *her*, did you? Because that would have been very hurtful.'

'I'm sure she's heard it already from the police,' I say. 'If they're looking for a motive, like she says they are.'

Jake shakes his head. 'There is no motive. Gus and Alina got on great, as far as I was aware. I'll phone the police and tell them that myself. And if they come around asking, you should say the same.'

'Of course,' I say. I don't know what he's so worried about, because there can't be any real evidence linking Alina to the nuts. No till receipt, no sign of nuts on her kitchen tools.

Which is a pity.

Can you send Jake down? Even allowing for what has happened, I think that's a bit rich.

*

As Jake said, the police phone to question me about Gus and Alina. They ask if I've ever heard any arguments between husband and wife, and I do exactly as Jake told me to.

'No, they got on really well. They were more likely to be laughing. Surely this was just some horrible freak accident?'

'Likely it was.'

'The only thing I can think of ...' I have a sudden idea. '*We* didn't know Gus had this allergy and we eat nuts all the time. They never said anything about touching things in the communal area – you know, handling post, that kind of thing. And delivery people and workmen come and go all the time. Any one of them might have brought traces of nuts into the house.'

'I'll make a note of that.' He asks if I've noticed any post going missing.

'Nothing in particular.' I remember what Jake said about the missing post, and I use it now: 'But you can't miss what you didn't know to expect, can you?'

'That's the problem,' the officer agrees.

There are no more questions.

Chapter 9

The funeral

The funeral is in the town on the coast where Gus grew up. I do not go. It's not the right thing to do – and not only because I am the one who caused the man's death. Gus didn't respect me. He made fun of me. He wasn't as hateful as Alina, but he wasn't my friend either.

Jake feels differently. He takes the day off work and travels with Alina in her little yellow car. They arrive in good time for the service so she can talk to the undertaker, and get ready to meet Gus's friends and family. I imagine Jake comforting her, as hymns are sung and people stand up and say what a tragedy it is that this promising young life has been cut short.

He comes back in the evening with a look of shame on his face, and I realize my images of their cosying up together were wrong. I know him, and it must have made him uneasy, being there as Alina's lover. He probably had to keep his distance from her in case people guessed he was more than just a neighbour – and that she was not quite the perfect wife she liked to present to the world.

'Hearing people speak about Gus made me feel like a bit of a fraud,' Jake says.

'How do you mean?' I ask. We're at the kitchen table, but he's not eating the M&S fish pie I've heated up. He drinks a beer in about ten minutes and gets himself a second.

I've moved the fern from the middle of the table and put a vase of roses in its place. The same pink as Alina's.

'I realized I didn't know him at all,' Jake explains. 'Not like they all did. There were all these amazing tributes.'

'What kind of things?'

'He did a lot of no-fee work and he raised money for charity – sponsored runs, that sort of thing. And he was funding his niece at university. He was one of the good guys, that's for sure.'

'Really?' I'm amazed. I had assumed he was selfish and vain, like Alina. It's on the tip of my tongue to say that, but I don't. Jake is looking guilty and unhappy enough as it is.

'I didn't even know his real name,' he says.

I glance up. 'His real name wasn't Gus?'

'Yes, but short for Angus. Angus Fletcher Hunt. Fletcher was his mother's maiden name.'

'Oh! Well, that explains that.' The letter I opened from the hospital was for him, not her. What an awful, careless mistake.

'Explains what?' Jake is looking at me oddly.

'Just that it makes sense about his name, because I'm sure I've seen post addressed to Mr A. Hunt.'

If only the allergy clinic had used the 'mister'!

Jake just shrugs.

'Did Alina cope all right?' I ask.

'Yes, she did well,' he says. 'I was proud of her.'

He's talking like he's her boyfriend. Has Gus's death brought them closer together? Now she's free, will he ditch me and move in with her? But, no. There's no way they can openly be a couple any time soon. Not while the police are sniffing around her. How long before it could look decent? A year, maybe.

A year is a long time, long enough for me to win him back. Maybe it's relief that makes me slip up a second time. 'It's such a mystery that Gus ate muesli just that one time.'

Jake frowns. 'What do you mean, just one time? Maybe he ate it a lot, but it was just that one batch that contained nuts.'

My heart thumps painfully. 'Sure, but he

always struck me as more of a bacon-sandwich kind of guy. She was the health freak, I thought, not him. But you're right. What do I know? I barely knew him. Maybe he'd eaten the same thing every day for years.'

Jake nods. 'Actually, Alina did say they'd just argued about him eating too much junk food. She gave him a hard time about having leftover pizza for breakfast, and she left in a bit of a mood. No wonder she's beating herself up about it.'

I piece together what I saw through the skylight with these extra details she's shared with Jake. They'd had breakfast and she told him off about the pizza. She left the flat and he made himself more coffee. Then he poured himself a bowl of muesli. He thought, *Maybe I will change my ways. No time like the present.*

So, in a way, this is Alina's fault.

Jake goes on: 'On top of everything else, she's had a letter from the police about some speeding ticket that never arrived. Turns out that if you don't respond in time, they fine you and take six points from your licence. Not a big deal compared to your husband dying, but those are things that can push you over the edge.'

'Poor thing,' I say. I don't like all this talk of missing post. It makes me think of that note I opened: *I know this is you*. It seems obvious Alina posted it to herself and meant for me to take it. Did she tell the police about it? Is that why they brought up the missing post when they phoned? Did she tell them I'm strange and envious, the sort of person to have a secret obsession with a neighbour?

What if the police decide to send an expert to my kitchen and they find traces of Brazil nuts? I've deep-cleaned the worktops and floors twice now, but there might still be the tiniest speck somewhere.

Suddenly, it seems an obvious plan for Alina to draw the police away from herself and onto me. I need to warn her off.

But first, I need to see Paula.

Chapter 10

Digging up the past

I phone Paula the next morning and ask if we can meet for lunch. We pick a café in Victoria, halfway between our offices, and sit together at a table in the window.

She leans forward to inspect me. 'You look exhausted, Simone. Is Jake still seeing that woman?'

'That's why I wanted to meet.' I keep my voice low. 'It's her husband. He's dead.'

The shock on Paula's face makes me feel fresh horror myself. *What have I done?*

'That's terrible! How did it happen? And when?'

'Just over two weeks ago. He had an allergic reaction and went into cardiac arrest.'

'I'm so sorry,' she says. 'You must feel really sad.'

'Yes.' I let my face droop. 'I didn't know him, but Jake says he was a really nice person. The thing is, Paula, you're the only one I've told about Jake's fling with Alina, and I don't want the police to know. It would confuse things.'

She blinks at me. 'Okay. I see that could look bad for Jake and this woman. But, don't worry, the police have no reason to talk to *me*, do they?'

'No. I just thought. In case they do, in the future.'

'Is he still seeing her?' she asks.

'He *sees* her. But I doubt they're doing anything. Whenever *I* see her, she's crying.'

Paula's eyes fill, even though she's never met these people. 'You have to have some sympathy for her, don't you? An allergic reaction is a horrible way to go. So sudden! No warning, nothing. One minute he's alive and healthy, the next gone. Was she with him when it happened?'

'No, he was on his own. It was me who saw him lying on the floor. I raised the alarm.' I repeat my lie about opening the bathroom window and seeing him through the skylight by pure chance.

She squeezes my hand. 'No wonder you're shaken, Simone! What a thing to witness. But at least, this way, his wife didn't find him dead on the kitchen floor when she came in from work.'

Paula starts to tell me about a colleague who is allergic to egg whites, and who was taken to A&E after shaking hands with someone who'd just eaten an egg mayo sandwich. She was saved, but suffered damage to her organs.

But all the time she's speaking, I can tell she's starting to think this through. She's wondering why I'm so keen to save the skins of two people who've hurt me so badly. She's thinking it'd be more like me to want to hurt them back.

She's remembering my dad's girlfriend. I wonder if Paula will say her name.

Suzi.

'I was a child,' I say with a sudden snap.

She flushes and I know I was right. 'Why do you say that?'

'Because I know what you're thinking. I did it *then*, so am I doing it again *now*? But I was a child,' I repeat. 'Mum and Dad split up and I blamed Suzi. I had a chance to hurt her and I took it. But it was twenty-five years ago, for God's sake!'

'All right,' Paula says, in a soothing voice. 'I know that. No need to get so upset about the past, Simone.'

Easy for her to say.

It was the first time my brother Matt and I had gone to stay with Dad and Suzi in the flat they'd moved into together. We'd been told by Mum we had to go every other weekend from now on, even though we didn't want to. Well, *I* didn't want to. Matt was three years older than me and I could tell he wasn't as bothered. He was getting sick of Mum crying all the time, and not cooking meals, or cleaning the house, or any of the other things she was supposed to do.

We arrived after school on Friday night. Suzi made lasagne and I knew Dad must have told her it was my favourite. It smelled delicious. It was hard not to eat a single bite, but I managed it.

Matt wolfed his down as if he hadn't eaten for weeks.

'Your mum not feeding you?' Dad said in a jokey voice.

'Yes, she is,' I answered for my brother. I allowed myself a few salad leaves.

'Don't go starving yourself like those anorexic types,' Dad told me.

Suzi pretended she wasn't hurt by my refusing to eat her food. 'What do you two want to be when you grow up?' she asked us, as if we were five years old.

'An undertaker,' I said, to shock her. But she just caught my dad's eye and they laughed together in a way that showed me he had warned her that I was strange.

'What about you? I bet you're not quite so dark as your sister,' she said to Matt.

He shrugged. He found Suzi difficult because she was blonde and curvy – I'd heard him tell friends she was sexy. 'A footballer,' he said, with his mouth full.

'Who do you support?'

'Man United.' And just like that, he was chatting to her as if she hadn't ruined Mum's life. *Our* lives.

'I'm going to bed,' I said.

'So early?' said Dad. 'We thought we could all watch a film together?'

'No thanks.'

They'd put bunk beds in the tiny second bedroom – like I said, as if we were five. The walls were thin and I could hear them laughing at the film. They had sweets or chocolates or something, and Suzi called out things like, 'Hey, who ate all the purple ones!' She was so fake.

The next morning, Matt was still asleep in the bottom bunk when I climbed down. In the kitchen, Dad and Suzi were standing close together by the fridge, and sprang apart when they saw me.

'Can I get you some orange juice?' Suzi asked. It was annoying that she was the one to ask, because if it had been Dad I could have said yes. But since it was her, I had to say no.

'I'll get myself some water,' I muttered.

'You can't go on a hunger strike every time you stay with us,' Dad said.

'I'm not on a hunger strike.'

'Well, that's what it looks like.'

I scowled at him and he lost his temper. 'Stop being so rude to Suzi!'

'It doesn't matter,' Suzi said.

'It does,' Dad barked, and I was pleased I'd made them disagree.

'Let's give her a bit of space,' Suzi said. She sounded calm, but I could tell I'd upset her because when they left the room she forgot to take her coffee with her and she'd only drunk a third of it.

I held her mug in my hand, feeling warmth pass through my cold fingers.

Then I had an idea.

Chapter 11

A warning for Alina

Paula and I part on good terms. We always do. But Alina will be much harder to manage, and for the rest of the day I think hard about how to do it. Martin doesn't seem to mind that I'm not doing much work. Every day since Gus died, someone in the team pats me on the shoulder or offers me a cupcake. They're all so sorry about the ordeal I've been through.

I decide a simple enquiry is a natural way to open matters. As soon as I get home, I knock at her door. There's no music or light coming from her flat, but she's always in now. She hasn't gone back to work since Gus's death. She's a recluse. I can hardly make her out at the kitchen table these days because she doesn't turn on the lights. She sits in the dark with a plate of food in front of her, lifting a fork to her mouth like a robot acting like a human.

There's a look of hope on her face when she

answers the door, but that changes when she sees me. She thought I was Jake.

'Hi, Alina. I just wanted to see how you're doing? Jake told me the funeral went smoothly.'

She invites me in, which is a first. I follow her down the hallway to the kitchen, noticing her dark shapeless clothes and bare feet. The lights snap on and I'm shocked by the mess – dirty dishes everywhere, an overflowing bin. You can see fluff and dust and hairs on the marble floor. My eyes find the spot where Gus fell.

'I haven't ever seen your extension,' I lie, because of course she doesn't know I have been here before. 'Jake has, of course.'

This is my first warning to her, but she ignores it. 'Gus helped design it,' she says. 'He knew exactly what he wanted. Everyone assumed I was the one with the eye for interiors, but it was him. He chose the kitchen units, the sofa, everything.'

'Did he choose the bed?' I ask. My second warning.

'What?'

I smile. 'I saw it through your bedroom window once. That huge bamboo headboard!'

She accepts this. 'Thank you. It *was* his, yes. He had it in his old flat before we got married. It came from a flea market in France.'

She makes tea and puts biscuits on a small

plate. 'They're nut-free, but I suppose I don't have to be so careful now. I could have a big bowl of Brazil nuts in every room and it wouldn't matter.'

This seems like a good time to ask about the police. 'How is it going with the case? Have they discovered anything new?'

'Not really. It's hard to prove how the nut got into the muesli. They've been talking to the company that makes it, but they deny everything. They say there hasn't been a single other incident or complaint. They're a small firm and they really don't need the bad press.'

As she speaks, my eyes stray to the wedding photo of Gus and her. I imagine her standing in front of it, touching his face with her fingers and crying.

'The police do know the nut was finely ground and they can probably narrow down which kind of grinder was used. I've told them I don't own one, but what does that matter?' She gives a grim laugh. 'I could have thrown it away after I'd done the deed.'

I think of my own grinder, long crushed in a bin lorry or buried in a tip. Where did I get it from? I think it was a gift from my old boss, who used to do a raffle at Christmas. No receipt, no trail.

'My solicitor says to be patient,' Alina adds with

a sigh. 'It will be a dead end. I hope so. The only vaguely suspicious thing is the missing post.'

She looks at me then, and I know I was right to come here and warn her off. I take a deep breath. 'The police asked me about that, too, but I don't think they see it as important. They spent far more time on other questions.'

She angles her head, watching me. 'What other questions?'

'About you and Gus.' I hold her gaze. 'But don't worry, I didn't say anything.'

'What do you mean? What *could* you have said?' There's a trace of her old superiority when she says, 'Spit it out, Simone.'

'They asked if there were any problems between you.'

'And?'

'I said no.'

'Good. Because there weren't.'

I don't like the rude way she's speaking to me now. I need to make myself clearer. 'I mean, I *could* have said he was away quite a bit, and that you often had guests for dinner on those nights. Male guests. Then again, absence makes the heart grow fonder in a lot of cases. I find that myself, when Jake works late. I can't wait for him to get home. I almost think I can hear his voice before he actually arrives. Crazy, isn't it?'

Her shoulders go rigid and her face turns ugly with fury – and fear. She knows exactly what I'm saying. 'Absence makes the heart grow fonder? Is that *really* the right thing to say to someone who's just buried her husband? Telling me how much you miss *your* man when mine's just died?'

I smile sadly at her. 'You're right. I'm sorry. Anyway, the police will find their own answers, I'm sure. They don't need my silly ideas.'

She looks at me with hatred. 'I think you should go.'

I rise to my feet. 'I think I should.'

She must have phoned or texted Jake as soon as I left, because when he gets back from work, he only comes upstairs to tell me he needs to go straight back down again.

'Alina's in a bad way,' he says.

'You don't have to explain,' I say, coolly. 'I just spoke to her myself and she made it quite clear her claim is greater.'

This annoys him. 'What does that mean?'

It means I'm getting tired of this love triangle. It means things are coming to a head, like it or not. 'It means you've spent more time with her recently than you have with me,' I tell him. '*You* might think it's the right thing to do, to be at her beck and call, but that doesn't mean *I* do.'

He takes a step towards me, his face pained. 'Simone, she's our neighbour and she's been through the most horrific event. Imagine if it was me who'd just dropped dead. You'd be in a bad way too.'

If that was the case, Gus wouldn't be up here looking after me, I think. But then I remember what Jake said about all the tributes at his funeral. *He was one of the good guys* ... And I killed him! I have a sudden, dizzy feeling that none of this is really happening and we are all actors speaking lines written by someone else.

'Just go,' I say, at last, and he sighs and turns, closing the door gently behind him.

Two minutes later, I go up to the bathroom and look down at the skylight. Alina is sitting at the table with her head in her hands, in Gus's seat. Jake is there too. I watch as he drops to his knees to plead with her, then moves out of sight. He comes back with a beer and sits next to her, their heads close together as they speak. She'll be telling him what I said. She'll be saying I suspect them. That I've threatened her.

They talk for a long time, long enough for the sky to darken and for me to start to feel hungry. Then, quite suddenly, Jake lifts his face to the skylight. I know he can't have caught any movement from my window, so perhaps he saw a bird or heard a noise of some sort. Whatever it was, he's staring blindly into my eyes. And as I stare back, I know he's working it all out. The room at the top he never uses, the window he's never looked out of. Alina must have told him what I said about him having seen her flat, and about her male guests when Gus was away. Maybe about the bed, because they *never* open their bedroom blind.

Jake gets to his feet and says something to Alina. She follows and they stand side by side, both looking up. My breath falters. The hairs on my arms rise. This is *eerie*.

As I finally breathe out again, Jake springs out of view, towards the door. I know what he's about to do. He's going to dash up here and see with his own eyes what it is that I can see.

I act fast. I'm down the stairs to my flat door in seconds. The key is in the lock and I turn it, pulling the security bolt for good measure. Five seconds later, he thunders up and I hear his key scraping in the lock.

'Simone, unbolt the door!'

I don't move.

'I know you're there!' His voice sounds so different, it's like a stranger saying my name. I can't speak. I'm focused on my own breathing. Four beats in, four beats out.

'What's going on?' he demands. 'Why've you locked yourself in?'

I find my tongue. 'Go away. I want to be on my own.'

Now Alina's voice comes from the hall downstairs: 'Simone, come out! We need to talk to you.'

'I have nothing else to say to you, Alina. You just threw me out of your flat! You've had your chance, now keep the hell away from me.'

That shuts them up. I can hear them whispering together. Then Jake speaks again: 'You can't lock me out. I live here! Where am I supposed to sleep tonight?'

'Sleep downstairs,' I yell. 'I'm sure *she* won't mind.'

'*I* mind!' But he gives up soon enough and goes downstairs.

I pour a glass of wine and try to stay calm. I ignore the phone calls from him and refuse to listen to the voicemail. He switches to texts:

Let's talk tomorrow. After work?

Simone? This is crazy.

Tomorrow? Please!

I make him wait till almost midnight before answering:

Fine. Tomorrow 7pm.

In the bathroom, when I look down at her kitchen, I can't see a thing. At first, I think it's because the lights are out but, when my eyes adjust, I make out a large square of faintly glowing grey.

There is a dark sheet pinned over the skylight.

Chapter 12

Cards on the table

The next evening, Jake is already in when I come home from work. I know exactly where to find him, even before he calls out a greeting. The top bathroom.

He turns from the window as I enter and the look on his face is as flat as the glass behind him. 'All this time, you've had a direct view of them,' he says.

I shrug. 'This window overlooks their extension, yes.'

'But why didn't you tell them that when they put the skylight in?' he asks. 'You know they would have assumed this glass was opaque.'

'They didn't ask,' I say. 'They had no interest in anyone's opinion but their own.'

He gives a dry chuckle. 'The irony is, they asked *me*. A few months ago. Not about this window, but the one in my shower room with normal glass. I told them I couldn't see a thing because of the angle. It didn't occur to us this one had a clear view.'

'For God's sake, you make it sound as if I sit here all day long with a pair of binoculars,' I snap. 'I've got better things to do with my time, believe it or not. Like a full-time job.' I draw breath, remind myself to stay calm. 'I assume Alina told you what I said about her having visitors when Gus was away? Was that what made you guess?'

'It was that on top of other things,' Jake says. 'Things you said that stuck in my mind.'

'Like what?' I'm interested to know. I thought I'd kept my secret well.

'The fact that you saw Gus lying on the floor struck me as weird. You said you saw through the open window, but it was such a cold, wet day, it seemed odd that you'd have the window open more than a crack, if at all. And that comment you made about the muesli. How could you know he'd only tried it once? Only if you were in the habit of watching him eat breakfast.'

'You're quite the Sherlock Holmes,' I say. 'Except it's hardly a crime knowing what someone ate for breakfast. I phoned for help when I saw he was unconscious – I'd call that being a good citizen.'

'But all the times before that,' Jake persists. 'It was a gross invasion of their privacy, Simone.'

I can't bear his pious tone. 'If you ask me, sleeping with my boyfriend is a gross invasion of *my* privacy.'

'Ah.' He dips his head.

'Don't deny it,' I say, sharply.

'I'm not going to. Shall we go down to the living room and talk? We can't stand in the bathroom all night.'

We sit on the sofa with a big space between us. The lamp light is soft and yellow, giving a glow to his face as I look at him.

'Turn your phone off,' I say, seeing him fiddling with it in his lap. I can't bear the thought of texts arriving from her while we talk. *How's it going? Does she know? Come back soon!*

'It's on silent,' he says, which I don't believe, but at least he puts it on the shelf out of reach. 'Simone, shall we agree that there's no point having this conversation unless we're both going to be a hundred per cent honest?'

I nod.

'So, ask me anything. You obviously know Alina and I have got closer than we should.'

'How did it start?' I ask.

'By accident, I suppose.' He has a look of wonder on his face. 'We got talking in the street one day and she invited me in. She was hard to resist.'

I scoff at this, but he protests. 'Honestly! I'm not sure I knew what was happening until it was too late.'

He means he'd never had a woman who looks as good as her come on to him. She was out of his league. I decide not to share my belief that Alina seduced him to spite me. Why she wanted it to continue, I'm not so sure.

'It wasn't just that once, though, was it? It's been an affair.'

'Yes, you're right,' he says. 'We became close. I don't think we expected to.'

In other words, he grew on her. Gus kept going away for work, and Jake was right there to take his place. And then Gus went away for good . . .

I can see Jake thinks that just by telling the truth he makes the acts behind the words all right. That it will soothe my anger and sadness. But he's wrong. It makes me want to provoke him. 'So have you told the police about it?' I ask.

That shocks him. 'I don't see how it would be relevant.'

'It's relevant because it's the missing motive,' I say.

'Missing motive?'

'Yes.' He's not such a Sherlock Holmes any more, I think. He takes me for a fool. 'It could be her reason to want to get rid of Gus. She'd lined up someone she liked better.'

'She didn't like me better,' Jake says.

'That might not be how the police see it. I'd say the fact that she hasn't been honest from the start makes it look even more suspicious.'

The look on his face tells me this is exactly what he and Alina feared. He stops playing dumb. 'It would be just as much of a motive for me as her, don't you think? I had a reason to want to get rid of Gus. I had access to the flat. I could easily have added the nuts to their cereal when Alina was out of the room. But you don't want me to be arrested, do you?'

We stare at each other. 'No,' I admit.

He sighs. 'Simone, you need to believe me when I say that since Gus's death, there's been nothing between Alina and me other than friendship. There was no way we could continue. We both wish it had never started in the first place. Alina feels really guilty.'

I search his face for clues. 'But you're down there all the time.'

His gaze softens. 'As a friend. She needs support, a shoulder to cry on. I know you two rub each other up the wrong way. But she's actually very grateful that you've been so patient about me being there for her. Especially on the day of the funeral. That was very difficult to cope with and she's not close to her family.'

I'm about to say that's no surprise, but then I remember that I'm not close to my brother. Without Paula, I'd have no family.

Jake moves closer to me. 'Is there any way you can forgive me? I promise you I've never done anything like this before and I never will again. Can we go back to how it was? Before all this awful drama. This tragedy.'

Well, this is exactly what I would like. To forget I ever found out about him and Alina, to forget I played a part in killing a man. 'What about her? You just said she needed you.'

'We talked about it last night, and she's going to ask a friend to come and stay, just while she sorts herself out.' He pauses. 'She's going to sell the flat – as soon as the police have closed their inquiry and let her get on with her life. It's too sad for her to stay in the home she shared with Gus. She misses him.'

I can't believe what he is saying. Is it really possible our mistakes will simply melt away?

'Where will she go?'

'Somewhere closer to work, she says. She might

rent in London for a bit while she decides. The point is, you would never have to see her again. And nor would I.'

Jake fetches us both a glass of wine and there is optimism in his face when he returns, a sense of progress between us.

'Why didn't you tell me you saw us through the skylight?' he asks. 'You could have stopped it much sooner.'

'*You* could have stopped it,' I correct him.

'You know what I mean. Tell me. Tell me what was running through your mind the first time you saw me down there.'

I want to be truthful, with myself as much as with him. 'I needed to see if it was going to continue. Then, when I knew it was, I didn't want to force you to choose.' My voice cracks, the most emotion I've shown so far. 'I was scared you would choose her.'

'I would never have done that,' he says. 'It's over. I want to commit to this, Simone. To us.'

It occurs to me he might be saying all this because it's over with her. Alina has finished with him, and he's making up to me because he has no choice. He has nowhere else to go. I should tell him I have this doubt. I should tell him I'm not someone he can use. And yet ... Maybe I *can* accept that. I've committed my own crimes, and mine are bigger. If he stays here, we can win each other back.

'I'd like to get married,' I say. 'Not right now, but that's what I want for us, if we do try again.'

'OK. Good to know.' He is kissing me now. Kissing me like I imagine he kissed her. He is pulling at my clothes, making me have wild and swooping feelings.

'Shall we go upstairs?' I say.

'No, let's stay here.'

Knowing the layout of the bedroom downstairs as I do, I judge we are directly above Alina's bed as we have sex. It feels lovely, like it used to when we first got together. When it is over, Jake whispers the words into my hair:

'I have to know, Simone.'

'Know what?'

He pulls back and looks me in the eye. 'Was it you? Did you open the letter from the hospital?'

I go stiff. 'What letter?'

'I think you know. Did you think it was Alina who had the allergy? Because you thought his initials were hers? Did you add the nuts to her cereal?'

I open my mouth, but no words come out. No breath comes out, either. My heart drums scarily fast.

'It's okay, you can tell me. I know you would

never hurt anyone on purpose. It was a terrible accident. Tell me,' he urges. 'I've been honest about what I did wrong, now it's your turn. I want to support you, but I need to know what to say, what to hide.'

'I just . . . I just wanted to scare her,' I stutter. 'That was all. A stomach ache, a few days feeling unwell. I wanted her to feel pain.'

'How did you get into their flat?' Jake asks. 'Do you have a key?'

'No. When they had the builders in, I snuck in.'

'And you put the nut in the muesli box?'

'Yes.'

'Wow. And then you were the one who saw Gus fall ill. You must feel worse than any of us.'

'I do!'

He pulls me closer and I feel the tension ease. He understands how it was, how it went horribly wrong.

'I wish I could go back,' I cry. 'I would do anything to be able to make it go away. Make Gus come back.'

'I know,' he says, gently.

'Has she guessed, as well?' I ask.

'Alina? No, absolutely not.'

'You won't tell her?'

He squeezes me. 'I'm not going to tell anyone. We have to forget this. Start again as if we never knew either of them. Let's agree that we don't ever talk about it again.'

I want nothing more. 'I'm not a murderer, Jake,' I cry.

'Of course you're not. I can't have a murderer for a wife.'

I breathe out. He is back. He is mine again. I've been given a second chance.

Actually, it's a third.

Chapter 13

Suzi's story

The day after Jake and I reunite is the happiest since this began. The first one in months when I wake feeling peaceful. No headache, no racing pulse, no rash on my neck. I am calm and able to face the future. I have Jake back. Alina is not going to get in trouble for a crime she didn't commit, and I am not going to get in trouble for the one I did.

I wonder how soon the flat will go on the market and how long it will take to sell. Not very long, I'm guessing. It's big and beautiful and has that amazing skylight.

I imagine people moving around the rooms, touching things and asking, 'What are the upstairs neighbours like?' And the agent saying, 'Oh, very quiet. They keep themselves to themselves.'

I don't suppose he will tell them that a man died there.

'You're in a good mood today,' Martin says at work.

'I might be getting married,' I say.

'You *might* be?' He throws back his head. 'You make me laugh, Simone. But I'm happy for you. Really happy.'

After lunch, Paula phones. 'Have you looked at the BBC website this week?'

'No.'

'Scroll down the main page for "Suzi's Story". They do this thing where people write about a past trauma and say they've forgiven the person who hurt them. I think you might find it interesting.'

I bring up the website while she's on the line and soon find the piece.

My partner's daughter poisoned me

It was a few months after I'd started seeing Andrew when his two kids came to stay with us for the first time. I was nervous because I didn't have much experience with children. The son was a typical teen, a bit sullen, but quite sweet. The daughter was something else. She had a really chilling way about her and she made it clear she didn't like me. The evening didn't go well and when she went to bed early, I knew it was to avoid spending time with me.

The next morning, she came into the kitchen,

where Andrew and I were drinking coffee. They had a bit of an argument and we left her alone for a few minutes. I forgot my coffee, and when I went back to get it, I realized as soon as I drank it that there was something in it. It tasted foul! Andrew got it out of the girl that she'd put white spirit in it while we were out the room. We dashed to the hospital. I was in agony with cramps, but we got there quickly enough to get the contents of my stomach pumped and to avoid any real damage.

She didn't pull another stunt like that, but I could never relax in her presence. Andrew and I split up after a year or so. When you have that kind of reaction to a new relationship you have to be rock solid and we weren't. I think it would have been different if he hadn't had kids.

He died quite young, I heard. I don't know what happened to the daughter, but she'll be in her late thirties now. I worry sometimes that by turning a blind eye on that occasion I might have put someone else in danger. Maybe lots of people.

'Crazy,' I tell Paula. 'She must have done it for the money. Well, bully for her.'

There is a silence. 'Any news on Jake and the woman downstairs?' Paula asks, finally.

'Yes. He's stopped seeing her.'

'Thank God for that,' Paula says.

I decide not to mention getting married, because the article has put me in a bad mood. I wonder why she wanted me to read it. It's not like it includes my name. I would never have stumbled across it on my own.

I'm starting to have doubts about Paula. Have I told her too much?

I say a polite goodbye and end the call.

I remember Dad phoning Matt from the hospital with an update. He and Suzi had told the A&E doctors it was all a silly accident, that one of the kids had thought the white spirit was water. The staff had agreed not to inform the police.

'They're not going to tell Mum,' Matt said, as we took the bus back home. 'They think she's upset enough without knowing her daughter's a psycho.'

'I am not a psycho,' I said.

'You bloody are. I can't wait to get away from this family.'

'I can't wait for you to go,' I said.

When Suzi was well again, Dad met me from school and we went for a walk on our own.

'Do you know what could have happened, Simone? If she'd drunk any more of that stuff? If we hadn't got her to the hospital so fast? She could have gone into a coma. She could have died. You would have been sent to a prison for children, and you can take it from me that they are terrible places.'

I didn't reply, and he sighed and told me my older cousin Paula would be keeping an eye on me from now on. She lived in a nearby town and would check in on me every week. Be a kind of buddy to me.

'Do you understand what I'm saying, girl?'

'Yes,' I said, but he continued as if I hadn't agreed and he still needed to go on warning me.

'We're supporting you this time, but if you try anything like this again, it will be a different story. A very different story.'

Chapter 14

Plans for the future

That evening, Jake and I have dinner and he doesn't slip away to see Alina. In fact, we don't mention her. We talk about normal things, like where we should go on holiday. I show him a picture of a hotel in Italy with a lake like a mirror, soaring green mountains and couples who were made for each other.

I don't say anything about Paula's phone call or the article by Suzi. Soon some other hard-luck story will be in that space. When I was young, Paula used to tell me I had to give people the benefit of the doubt. Now I'm going to apply that to her. She is my friend, not my enemy, just like Jake.

As I brush my teeth before bed, I don't even look down at the skylight, not even to check if it's still covered. The habit is broken, the habit that caused so much tragedy. I wonder if I should find out from Jake where Gus is buried, and go and put some flowers on his grave. Try to say I'm sorry.

Maybe when Alina has moved away. For now, I will arrange for the bathroom window to be changed. I will ask for the bottom half to be frosted and the top half clear. That way, I'll be able to see the sky, but not the skylight.

'That's a good idea,' Jake says, when I tell him.

The next day is Friday. It's been an intense week and I'm looking forward to the weekend. Jake suggests we go down to the south coast tomorrow. Walk on the beach, eat fish and chips. Forget all about Gus and Alina. Forget about death.

'I'll look at train times,' he says.

He's about to leave for work when the doorbell goes. 'Must be the postman.'

I don't bother saying that the postman never comes this early. He comes in the middle of the day when we're all out. I think of the mail I stole, including the wedding invitation. Was Alina ever sent another? Will she go on her own or will it be too sad, without Gus? Make her think too much about *their* wedding. When Jake and I get married, there's no way we will frame a massive photo of ourselves like they did. Showing off like celebrities.

I note the mean thought and stop myself having another one. I think of the different, better ways I could have handled my anger. I hear Paula's voice telling me, *No need to get so upset about the past.*

I will say this to myself every day now, like a prayer, to remind myself.

'Simone?' Jake is calling to me from the hallway. His voice is serious now, and urgent. 'You need to come!'

'Okay!' I hurry out just as two uniformed police officers arrive at the open flat door. 'What's going on?'

'I'm not sure,' Jake says.

After checking my name, one of the officers pulls out handcuffs and says to me: 'I am arresting you on suspicion of murder. You do not have to say anything, but it may harm your defence ...' I hardly hear the rest, but I've heard it hundreds of times before on TV, so it doesn't matter.

It basically means they know. They've worked it out.

'Jake?' I wait for him to protest, to stand up for me, but he doesn't say a word. The look on his face is completely wrong. He isn't at all upset. He is grim. Bag over his shoulder, phone in his hand, he looks ready.

I see it all in that moment. He didn't want to win me back. He wanted to get rid of me. Yesterday, while I was telling Martin I was getting married, he was telling the police I was a killer.

But don't they need evidence to make an arrest like this? This is his word against mine! I find my voice: 'Whatever this man has told you, he's lying. He's been having an affair with Alina. They must have killed Gus and set me up!'

But I sound shrill and feeble, and no one replies. One of the officers says that we are ready to leave and he leads the way down the stairs. As I follow, I see Jake draw his phone to his chest. It's just a little gesture, but enough for me to understand. He must have recorded our conversation. My confession.

I just wanted to scare her.

I wanted her to feel pain.

At the foot of the stairs, I am aware of Alina standing in her doorway, watching us. Her eyes meet mine and hatred pours towards me, a dark, filthy torrent of it. I watch as Jake goes to stand next to her, his arm around her waist. Then the front door is opening and I am stepping into daylight. I'm not wearing a coat and the cold air goes through my clothes and touches my skin.

'Throw away the key,' Alina calls after us, her voice angry, and I shiver.

The police car is parked to the left, outside the gate of number 19. In our spot is a big white van with huge letters on the side: 'Surrey Skylights'. Three workmen smoke cigarettes as they watch us go by.

'Busy morning, eh? Leave the gate open,' one of them says, and I see Alina come out to greet them.

I get into the back of the police car and strain to catch a final glimpse of Jake through the open door. But the van doors swing open and block my view. The men begin unloading a huge sheet of opaque glass and Alina steps aside to let them pass.

'I wouldn't want to be the one to drop *that*,' says the police officer at the wheel.

'I wouldn't want to be the one standing under it when you do,' says the one in the passenger seat, and they chuckle like a pair of idiots. They think they're so funny.

But all I can think is how ironic it is. Alina could have kept her clear skylight after all, because I will no longer be there to watch her through it. Or the people who live there after her.

At last, after a final flash of sunlight on glass, the engine starts and we pull off.

The police station is not far away.

Acknowledgements

Thank you to the Quick Reads team, including commissioning editor Fanny Blake, literacy editor David Reynolds, and of course Jojo Moyes for making this year's collection possible. The Simon & Schuster team has been a joy to work with on this project, including Suzanne Baboneau, Alice Rodgers, Jess Barratt, Sara-Jade Virtue and Pip Watkins. Thank you to my agent Sheila Crowley at Curtis Brown, as well as Sabhbh Curran and Emily Harris. Also, a special thanks to Alice Lutyens at Curtis Brown, who many years ago mentioned how easy it is (in some cases) to spy through a neighbour's skylight – I never forgot that comment!

About Quick Reads

"Reading is such an important building block for success"
- Jojo Moyes

Quick Reads are short books written by best-selling authors. They are perfect for regular readers and those who are still to discover the pleasure of reading.

Did you enjoy this Quick Read?
Tell us what you thought by filling in our short survey. Scan the QR code to go directly to the survey or visit https://bit.ly/QuickReads2021

Turn over to find your next Quick Read...

A special thank you to Jojo Moyes for her generous donation and support of Quick Reads and to Here Design.

Quick Reads is part of The Reading Agency, a national charity tackling life's big challenges through the proven power of reading.

www.readingagency.org.uk
@readingagency   #QuickReads

The Reading Agency Ltd. Registered number: 3904882 (England & Wales)
Registered charity number: 1085443 (England & Wales)
Registered Office: Free Word Centre, 60 Farringdon Road, London, EC1R 3GA
The Reading Agency is supported using public funding by Arts Council England.

Supported using public funding by
ARTS COUNCIL ENGLAND

THE READING AGENCY

Find your next Quick Read:
the 2021 series

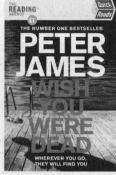

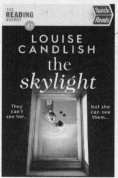

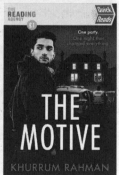

Available to buy in paperback or ebook and to borrow from your local library.

More from Quick Reads

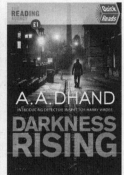

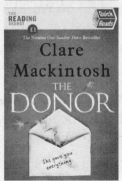

For a complete list of titles and more information on the authors and their books visit

www.readingagency.org.uk/quickreads

Continue your reading journey

The Reading Agency is here to help keep you and your family reading:

Challenge yourself to complete six reads
by taking part in Reading Ahead
at your local library, college or workplace
readingahead.org.uk

Join Reading Groups for Everyone to find a
reading group and discover new books
readinggroups.org.uk

Celebrate reading on World Book Night
every year on 23 April
worldbooknight.org

Read with your family as part of the
Summer Reading Challenge
at your local library
summerreadingchallenge.org.uk

For more information, please visit our website:
readingagency.org.uk

the
other
passenger

Enjoyed
The Skylight?

Turn the page for an extract from
Louise Candlish's brand-new novel

1

27 December 2019

Like all commuter horror stories, mine begins in the mean light of early morning – or, at least, *officially* it does.

Kit isn't there when I get to St Mary's Pier for the 07.20 river bus to Waterloo, but that's not unusual; he's had his fair share of self-inflicted sick days this festive season. An early-morning sailing calls for a strong stomach at the best of times, but for the mortally hungover it's literally water torture (trust me, I know). In any case, he always arrives after me. Though we live just five minutes apart and he passes right by Prospect Square to get to the pier, we gave up walking down together after the first week, when his spectacularly poor timekeeping – and my neurotic punctuality – became apparent.

No, Kit prefers to stroll on just before they close the gangway, raising his hand in greeting, confident I've secured our preferred seats, the portside set of four by the bar. At St Mary's, boarding is at the front of the boat and so I'll watch him as he moves down the aisle, hands glancing off the metal poles – as much for style as balance – before sliding in next to me with an easy grin. Even if he's been up late partying, he always smells great, like an artisan loaf baked with walnuts and figs ('Kit smells so *millennial*,' Clare said once, which was almost certainly a criticism of me and my Gen X smell of, I don't know, stale dog biscuits).

Get us, he'll say, idly scanning the other passengers, snug in their cream leather seats. It's one of his catchphrases: *Get us*. Pity the poor saps crushed on the overland train or suffocating on the Tube – *we're* commuting by *catamaran*. Out there, there are *seagulls*.

Also, sewage, I'll reply, because we've got a nice sardonic banter going, Kit and me.

Well, we used to.

I clear the lump in my throat just as the boat gives a sudden diesel rumble, as if the two acts are connected. On departure, information streams briskly across the overhead screens – *Calling at Woolwich, North Greenwich, Greenwich, Surrey Quays* – though by now the route is so imprinted I pay little attention. Through the silver sails of the Thames Barrier and past the old aggregate works and industrial depots of the early stretch; then you're at the yacht club and into the dinghy-strewn first loop, the residential towers of the peninsula on your left as you head towards the immense whitehead of the O2 Arena. Strung high above the river is the cable car that links the peninsula to the Royal Docks, but I won't allow myself to think about my only trip to date on *that*. What was done that night. What was said.

Well, maybe just briefly.

I turn my face from the empty seat beside me, as if Kit is there after all, reading my mind with its secret, unclean thoughts.

'Back again on Friday,' he grumbled on the boat on Monday night, bemoaning his firm's insistence on normal working hours for this orphan weekday between Boxing Day and the weekend. 'Fucking cheapskates.' Normally, if he misses the boat, I'll text him a word of two of solidarity: *Heavy night?* Maybe some beer emojis or, if I was involved in the session, a nauseated face. But I don't do that today. I've hardly used my phone since before Christmas and I admit I've enjoyed the break. That old-school nineties feeling of being incommunicado.

We're motoring now past the glass steeples of Canary Wharf towards Greenwich, the only approach that still has the power to rouse my London pride: those twin domes of the Old Royal Naval College, the emerald park beyond. I watch the bar staff serve iced snowflake cookies with the teas and coffees – it's surprising how many people want to eat this stuff first thing in the morning, especially my age group, neither young enough to care about their silhouette (such a Melia kind of word) nor close enough to the end to give a damn about health warnings. Caffeine and sugar, caffeine and sugar: on it goes until the sun is over the yardarm and then, well, we're all sailors in this country, aren't we? We're all boozers.

Only when we dock in front of the *Cutty Sark* do I finally reach for my phone, reacquaint myself with my communications of Monday night and the aftermath of the water rats' Christmas drinks. I scan my inbox for Kit's name. My last text to him was spur-of-the-moment and tellingly free of emojis:

Just YOU wait.

Sent at 23.38 on Monday, it's double-ticked as read, but there has been no reply. There *have* been, however, five missed calls from Melia, as well as three voicemails. I really should listen to them. But, instead, I hear Clare's voice from yesterday morning, the 'proper' talk we had under a gunmetal northern sky four hundred miles from here:

You need to cut ties.

Not just him, Jamie. Her, as well.

There's something not right about those two.

Now she tells me. And I slip the phone back in my pocket, buying myself a few extra minutes of innocence.

LOUISE CANDLISH

those people

Meet the neighbours you'll love to hate.

Until Darren and Jodie move in, Lowland Way is a suburban paradise. Beautiful homes. Friendly neighbours. Kids playing out in the street. But Darren and Jodie don't follow the rules and soon disputes over loud music and parking rights escalate to threats of violence.

Then, early one Saturday, a horrific crime shocks the street. As the police go house-to-house, the residents close ranks and everyone's story is the same: *they* did it.

But there's a problem. The police don't agree. And the door they're knocking on next is yours.

'Scarily plausible'
Observer

AVAILABLE NOW IN PAPERBACK AND EBOOK

**SIMON &
SCHUSTER**

LOUISE
CANDLISH

our
house

**Winner of Crime & Thriller Book of the Year 2019
at the British Book Awards**

*On a bright morning in the London suburbs,
a family moves into the house they've
just bought on Trinity Avenue.*

*Nothing strange about that. Except it's your house.
And you didn't sell it.*

When Fi Lawson arrives home to find strangers moving
into her house, she is plunged into terror and confusion. She
and her husband Bram have owned their home on Trinity
Avenue for years and have no intention of selling. How can
this other family possibly think the house is theirs? And
why has Bram disappeared when she needs him most?

'Terrifically twisty . . . hooks from the first page'
Sunday Times

AVAILABLE NOW IN PAPERBACK AND EBOOK

SIMON &
SCHUSTER